To my son, Anduin—EPD

In memory of Pedro María, my father—Y

The Mysterious Stones

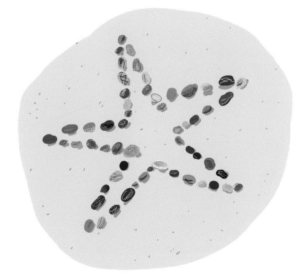

First published in 2020 by

CROCODILE BOOKS

An imprint of Interlink Publishing Group, Inc.

46 Crosby Street, Northampton, Massachusetts 01060

www.interlinkbooks.com

Text copyright © 2020 by Enrique Pérez Díaz • Illustrations copyright © 2020 by Yayo

English translation copyright © 2020 by Alina Ruiz

Published simultaneously in Canada by Tradewind Books, Vancouver

Library of Congress Cataloging-in-Publication Data available

ISBN 978-1-62371-869-5 • hardback

Book design by Elisa Gutiérrez

The text of this book is set in Brother 1816.

Printed and bound in Korea on forest-friendly paper.

10 9 8 7 6 5 4 3 2 1

MIX
Paper from
responsible sources
FSC® C023083
FSC
www.fsc.org

The Mysterious Stones

Enrique Pérez Díaz • Illustrations by Yayo

Translated by Alina Ruiz

Crocodile Books, USA

An imprint of Interlink Publishing Group, Inc.

www.interlinkbooks.com

One night, Kiki dreamed about his *papá*
who had sailed away on the open sea.

When he woke up, he heard a mysterious song
floating through his window on a soft ocean breeze.

Kiki followed the song down to the rocky beach where a woman with long white hair was gathering stones.

When she saw him, she disappeared into the sea.

"*Abuela*, I saw a mysterious woman on the beach collecting stones," Kiki said. "But she suddenly disappeared."

"When I was a little girl, a mysterious woman on the beach gave me some beautiful stones," his grandmother said. "I called her the Lady of the Stones.

When my *mamá* became ill, I put the stones under her pillow. I thought they might help her get well."

"Did she get better?"
"Yes, she got well."

Later at the market, Kiki and his abuela bought *chayotes*, sugar apples, plums, cashews, limes, *loquats*, eggplants, carrots, bananas, pineapples, grapefruits and melons. Smells of celery and cilantro, ginger and turmeric, filled the air.

As they walked back, Kiki's abuela said, "Your papá will never forget you. He loves you and one day he'll return."

At dawn, Kiki went down to the sea to look for the woman with flowing white hair. A pelican and a dolphin came to meet him. Flying fish, shining with foam, danced on the waves.

"Where has the Lady of the Stones gone?" Kiki shouted.
But the sea did not answer.

One foggy morning, Kiki saw a ship with tall white sails beached on the shore.

The Lady of the Stones climbed down off the deck onto the sand, tall and pale, her hair blowing in the salty sea breeze.

By the seawall, Kiki found a small pile of beautifully colored stones. When he turned to thank the Lady of the Stones, she had vanished.

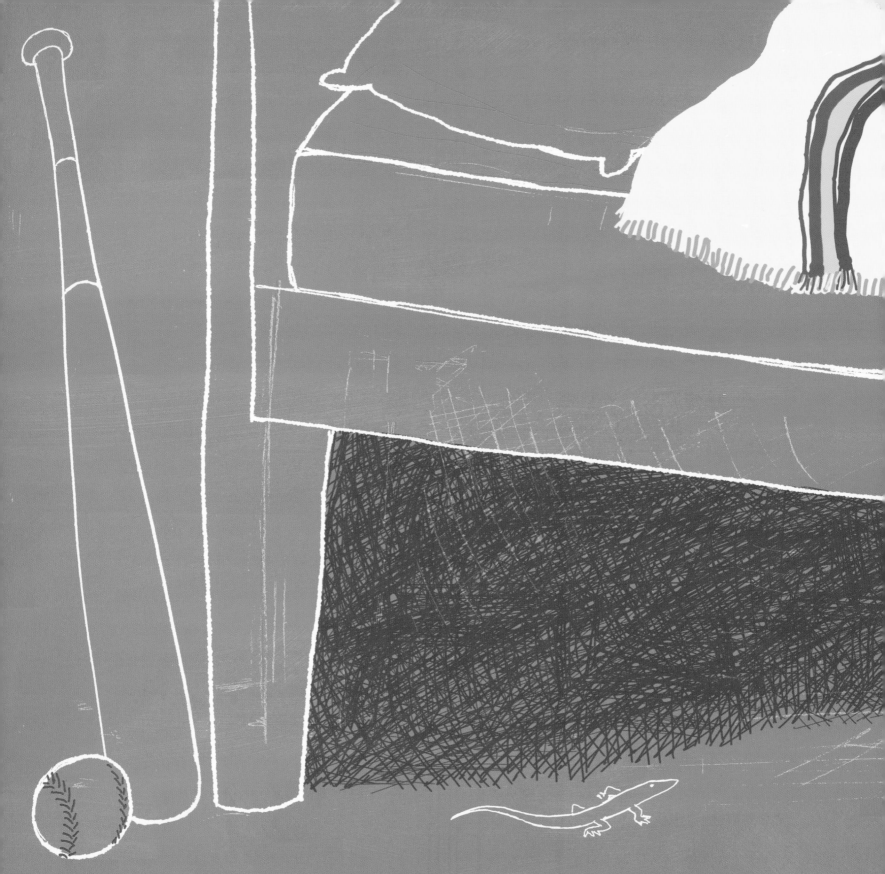

Kiki put the stones in a secret place.

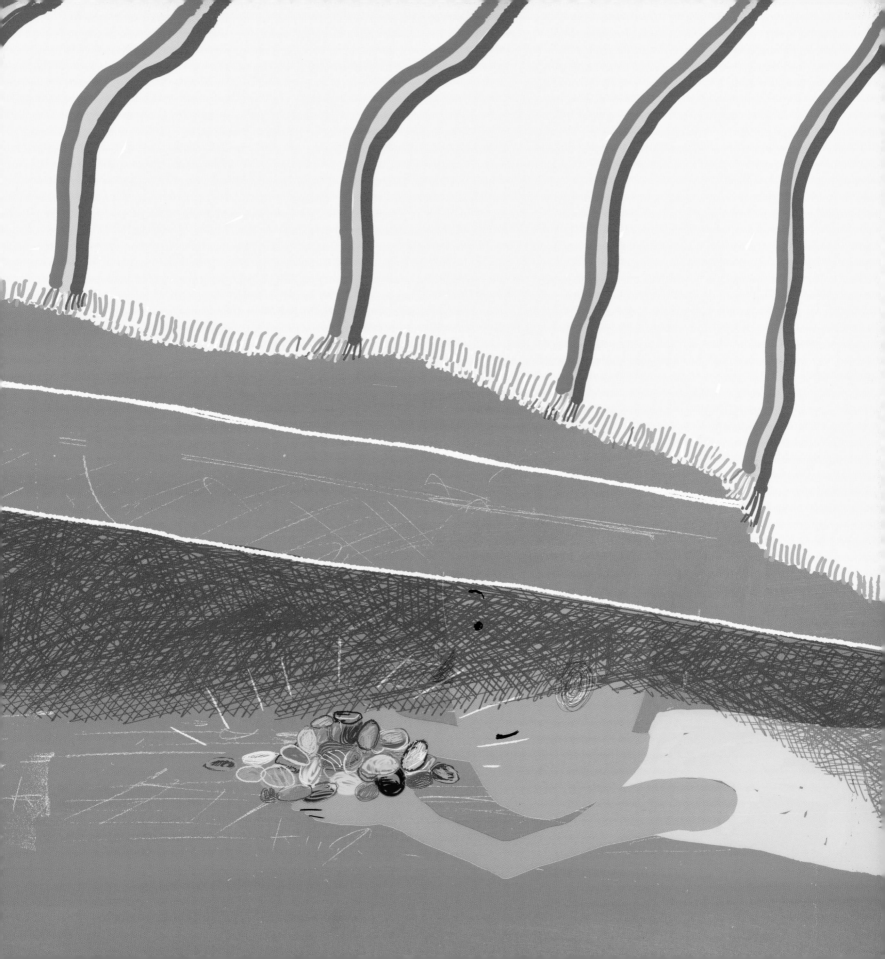

Later that day, out fishing with his *tío*, Kiki saw a sailboat appear far on the horizon. "Look at that boat!" he shouted. "It belongs to the Lady of the Stones!"

"I don't see anything," his uncle said. "It's just your imagination."

That evening, Kiki, his tío and abuela gathered around the kitchen table to eat salad, fried plantains, rice with black beans, and the fish Kiki and his tío had caught.

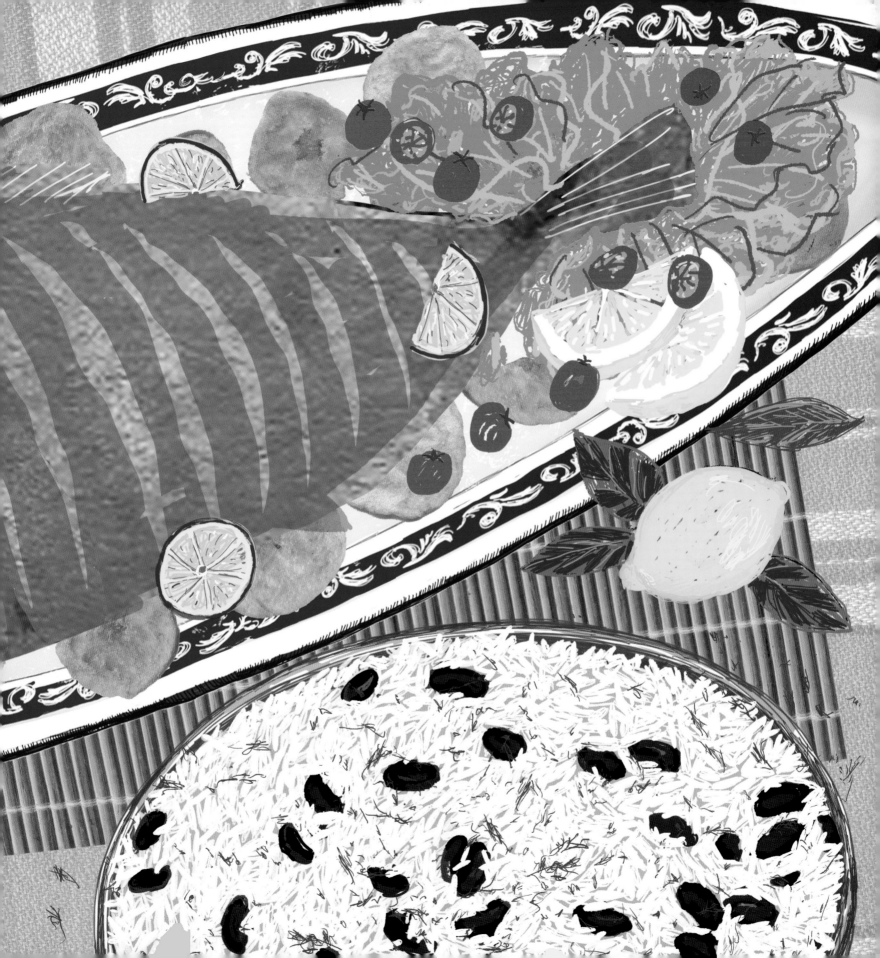

After dinner, Kiki fetched the stones of many colors and showed them to his abuela.

"The Lady of the Stones left these for me," he said.

His abuela took a jar of stones from the windowsill. "And these are the ones she gave me when I was little."

When the sun rose, Kiki went down to the shore and collected glass polished by the sea . . . so many colored crystals shining in the daylight!

He left them by the seawall.

"They are my gift for the Lady of the Stones."

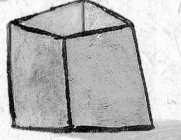

The next day, Kiki found a painted wooden box. Inside was
a glistening seashell, which he brought up to his ear.
Maybe it will tell me about my papá, he thought.
But he only heard the crashing of waves on the beach.

That night, in a dream, Kiki heard a voice in the seashell, "Never lose hope. Hope is a flower that blooms even in the deepest ocean."